5 Steps out of Depression

Dedication

I want to thank Tigger, Piper, Pumpkin, and Jenna for their company and support during my time and lessons throughout our years together. Time is the most valuable thing to share with a person. Only through them did I see myself through their eyes and realize the demons I had to fight within myself. Only with them did I see myself reflected through their own struggles. In each moment spent, we nurtured and helped me grow into the person I am today. I will never forget their presence or how they taught me to love. It is also through them and through their loss that I learned self-love and the strength to overcome so many obstacles. It was never time wasted, and with each, it was time fulfilled. They were all muse and an inspiration for many things. This essay is the result of their inspiration.

Contents

Five Steps Out of Depression

(Quick Reference Guide)

First Step:

Clean your self.

Clean your place.

-Organize your space

Make your bed.

Record your first day.

-start a journal

-how do you feel?

-Why are you doing this?

-What is your vision?

    -What are your spiritual Beliefs? If none, then maybe it's time to find them and start with that.

*Repeat daily and be thankful, and give yourself credit.

Second Step:

Move your body.

-Exercise, walk, shake

*Repeat daily and be thankful, and give yourself credit.

Third Step:

Do one thing that helps to improve your current status.

-Sobriety, if not sober (Drugs, even prescription fall under this heading)

-Therapy, just having someone to talk to on a regular basis will ensure success

-Work, if money is an issue

*Repeat daily and be thankful, and give yourself credit.

Fourth Step:

Add one more thing from step three when comfortable until all three are part of your daily or weekly habits.

*Repeat daily and be thankful, and give yourself credit.

These are all things we can control, and all steps will become second nature over a period of time. Continuous journaling will provide a reference of your thoughts and feelings each day. They will change over time and mark setbacks and success.

Fifth Step:

Remove anything and anyone who stands in the way of the four Steps.

This may require a move of household, town, or may require a bigger change. Friendships, situationships, or relationships can cause or contribute to your prolonged depression. This is a clean slate approach. Your history ends where you left it, and your new life and your new self await in a new place.

People will attempt to see you as you were and may not understand who you are becoming. You may not know who you are to become and a change in scenery is all that may be needed to assist in your journey.

*Repeat these steps as many times as necessary. Be thankful and give yourself credit for doing the work. This is the greatest work we can do; your future self will thank you. Be Brave.

Depression

There is a blankness, a hollow part of my soul. I cannot see it, yet I really feel it; it is there, and I know something must be there. All I can do is stare upward at the ceiling, sometimes at the wall. I never noticed before how thin the paint really is, I can see the seams of the spackle. There is this knowing that I am not alive, not dead, no thoughts. I am numb and cannot feel anything, but I hear all the ringing. It's gotten louder, I think. I lost track of time; what day is it? Is it night, are there stars, or is it sunny? I hope it rains so I can stay here.

I am sitting in a room with people. I know they are talking, but I do not know what is being said. There are sounds because I can feel the vibrations in my body. Is that music? I get up to go back into my room to lie down and I tell them I am just tired. I am not sure if I spoke those words aloud or just thought them in my mind. I go back to sleep, and that is all I can do. I am not hungry; do not feed me. I do not have the energy for utensils. I will sip water, but that requires effort.

Maybe just one more shot and it will get me drunk enough to turn off my thoughts. Nothing gets me drunk enough. I just do not want to think anymore. Maybe this time, I will finally smoke enough to be high again, like when I first started; everything was so happy then. I was happy then. Just one more oxycontin will kill the pain; it is in my heart this time and my muscles are so tense. You know I feel so confident when I take my anti-depressants, why can't they not last until bedtime? I do not like to have to feel anymore. I know it is a needle, but it is only a little. I can manage a little, and it's the only thing that works anymore. I am in control.

Depression is a deceptive mistress. You are only trying to cope with situations that have no solutions, but what does it take to return to life? The agony of emotions can be overwhelming sometimes, yet the real problem is that the causes of depression could have been ignored so long that it takes on a set of symptoms that are no longer on the surface.

Yet, these symptoms come out as lifestyle choices. Abandonment issues can turn into sex addiction. Grief and profound loss can become alcoholism. Prolonged sadness can become isolation.

I have experienced them all: abandonment, unrelenting grief, profound loss, and sometimes multiple losses within days and weeks of each other. Being bullied, ostracized, and completely isolated. I once drove on a highway through Nevada for 5 days without seeing a single person. Sometimes, there are prolonged bouts of feeling lifeless. I also experienced all the wrong ways of covering up the factual issues that created my chronic depression. Drugs, sex, alcohol, hyper-egotism, and self-destructive tendencies. Rage, and a general feeling of not caring about my own life or death, and at one time welcoming death.

The following essay is my solution for getting out of depression and all that once plagued and often stopped me from living my life. This is my pattern and system for getting out of depression. Life continues to challenge me, and I can say that my recovery time has shortened because of these steps. I have lived through many issues and continue to learn different things about why I do the things that I do. This is the great work. The most important work I could ever do. It is the greatest work any of us can do for the betterment of our lives. I strive continuously to find peace and happiness in everyday things. It does take time, and I do stumble. Once a person has had deep and profound experiences in their life that many would define outside of normal except able norms, that person is changed for the remainder of their life. These people can be an exception to many, and therefore, we all need to pay extra attention to how they conduct themselves within social norms. We all have a unique story to tell. Trauma is a term that gets thrown around to often and I feel it is a deceptive label. I am learning to let go of these labels for the sake of clarity. Labels tend to put things and people into a box. I do not fit into any box and never have, for that matter. I am unique, and my experiences are singular to my own choices. I take extreme care and accept responsibility for the things I have done. Perhaps this is part of a healing journey, I suppose. Depression is what I am attempting to address. Professional therapists are paid to assist with the memories of being hurt and can give us the language to use to define our feelings about those things. I want to show you a system for how to get to that point of "wanting" to get the help you need. A system to allow you to decide how and if you need help. How to take back your own life? How do you take control of your own journey? How to start? How do we start each day after falling, and how do we get back up if we fall again?

We will continue to have tests and trials for our entire lifetime. However, we can not depend upon others when they have not had the experiences or lived through some of the things we have. Those things we just cannot or don't want to talk about. Yes, it is great to develop and, at some point, have a support structure. Cheerleaders pep us up from time to time. What I am talking about is how do we help ourselves. So that when we do find the strength to seek friends and added support, we can choose those who help us and not attempt to keep us in a depressed state of existence.

There is a difference between real support and co-dependency. There is a difference between just being enabled and thriving. I want to thrive; I want to be able to look myself in the mirror and KNOW that I am in control of my reactions to situations and not just responding and dependent upon others. Healthy relationships are made when each person is an equal. Joe came in to work today wanting to do the dishes. Esteem needed to know that I am being the best version of myself. Equal footing is an understanding that each person has sometimes has separate dilemmas at different times, and being independent and knowing myself allows me to have the ability to support another person and visa versa and then be able to thrive, regardless of the events that come our way.

Depression can rob us of the ability to clearly see when we are being manipulated, coerced, or just simply unaware of the environment that we are living in. Depression can hide our ability to make decisions and may even determine a course of action that is counter to our own best interests. There may be situations where we have been in survival mode for so long that we don't even know we are depressed. The first time I learned about the condition and the label for depression was by accident. I was going through a very long period of bad events in my late teens after high school. The managers of the job I worked at kept a daily journal for the other as a record of all the things going on, including that of the employees. At this time, I was a full-blown alcoholic and experimenting with everything. A period in which I wrecked 5 cars in two- and one-half months. It never occurred to me that I was depressed until I read the words in the journal. It was something I was shown. I was one of the lead trainers for cooking. "Joe came into work today, wanting to do dishes. Still Depressed!" I remember it as a shot to my stomach. A short time after reading that entry and a very bad incident with acid, I started to investigate the possibility that I needed help.

Jim Carrey once defined depression as when your body decides that it is no longer able to live the character you are trying to portray. Then it shuts down, just like a computer crash. Now it is time to reboot, and in the following pages, that is exactly what I will attempt to show you. This system has worked for me over the years and continues to do so.

First Step

Let's get right to it. Depression varies from the event or the issue or condition that is put into this state. An event could be a death of a loved one. The breakup of a relationship is a series of unresolved feelings or issues. The most agreed-upon definition is that depression is a condition or mood disorder. It can be profound grief or sadness that can also be attributed to low self-esteem or self-loathing brought on by guilt. It's important to realize that feeling down at times is a normal part of life. Sad and upsetting events happen to everyone. But if you're feeling down or hopeless on a regular basis, you could be dealing with depression. Here is the first step towards recovery.

Clean yourself:

This may seem self-explanatory, but sometimes, after days of doing nothing but sleeping, lying and reflecting, we may have forgotten to do the simplest act of personal hygiene. It is often the simplest acts done with intention that will make a real difference in how you feel. Soaking in a bath or sitting in a shower for an extended time can be an act of renewal. Of course, we are not examining the causes of your sadness now, and they are not as important as getting started. After a few days or a week of consistent daily hygiene, try elevating this act into a focused pattern or even a ritual. Visualize all your concerns washing away with each soapy pass and allow the water to feel like more than a washing but as a way of cleansing the first layer of your being. You are rejuvenating and reinventing yourself anyway. Make it a sacred act from time to time. Today, this moment is the most important one: stay present.

There are different degrees of depression. Yet, regardless of what stage, degree, or length of your current bout with this, please understand the steps out of it are the same. Depression sometimes starts as a symptom of a bigger event or unresolved issue. Mild depression can be the result of a tragic event, a car crash, or the death of a loved one or pet. This form of depression can be easier to overcome and usually doesn't last exceptionally long. There are times when an unexpected event can last weeks or months. Again, check your progress as we go through each step. It is also especially important to talk about your feelings verbally. The more we talk about it, the less it stops us from being overwhelmed by the emotions behind the sadness. Often, there were situations when I was growing up where this was not an option, and as an individual, I had to isolate myself and work through my issues alone. This can be a go-to option when working on general problems, but not when it comes to depression. Moderate or reoccurring bouts of depression are an indication of an unresolved issue or past trauma. Journaling is a way to start to identify your feelings. Then, when it is still confusing, counseling of some sort is usually the solution. Lasting or chronic depression is a symptom of a major lifestyle issue. Repeated failings in relationships or the continuous need for medication, alcohol or drug use are good indicators of a severe problem. Drugs and alcohol are only momentary or temporary relief and should never be used to get through another day. This will hide your depression temporarily but will also cause a deeper and more pronounced form of depression. Remember, depression is a symptom and is not the end of your existence. I speak about this from personal experience. My problems only got worse and were even compounded by alcoholism and drug use. The illusions created from prolonged exposure only hid me from the grief I could not face. After years of losing loved ones, friends, and relatives, I turned coping into a lifestyle of living only for today, regardless of the consequences. The truth always finds a way back and not always in the most convenient time or place. I was also a traveler for many years; living on the road was also a way of life. A hot shower can be a miracle and a life-changing experience for the road-weary. After three days of not showering because of crying and hopelessness, a shower can also make you feel like a different person.

Clean your place:

You start with you, and now we will make our circle a little bigger in our environment. Some eastern cultures, like Japanese culture, have written volumes on this subject. Japanese consultant Marie Kondo promises that if you properly simplify and organize your home once, you'll never have to do it again. It is in this moment of cleaning that subconsciously we gain control over the external factors in our environment. Just like when you cleansed your body, now move outwards to your living conditions. If you live alone, I can almost guarantee there is a pile of dishes sitting in a sink and trash not taken outside. Our immediate living space is often the first causality when a bout of depression has taken our energy.

In depression, we cannot always see clearly what is going on around us or outside of our internal struggle. It is a condition of hopelessness that creates this mind-field, but it is an illusion. Our emotions have temporarily overwhelmed our thinking, and our understanding, and we are not sure what to do. It is like a corn maze where we cannot see over or past the next turn, and we don't know if that turn is going to get us out. So, we clean. Action is the answer. Stop thinking and start doing. Keep it simple. Clean you, then clean your space. Once cleaned, sit and look around for the change that you made. It will just immediately give you a sense of satisfaction and it is a visual reminder that change is possible. Baby steps are still steps. As you look around, focus on this feeling of accomplishment. Isn't this the exact thing you want to do? Take back control over your mind and life. Every step taken in this process is designed exactly to do that purpose. We can only control our responses to the events and challenges within our life experiences. Some things we cannot control, and with those, we can't get too attached and just accept to move on from the trial or lesson. I have a mantra, "it is what it is...."

When my immediate grandfather died, I was lost. I was named after him, and in growing up, he was the one who taught me how to respond to tragedy. My parents were divorced when I was nine, and my dad was only around on weekends. When I was ten, I was at my grandparents I got a phone call that one of my friends had died from heart failure. He suffered from asthma and at that time, doctors prescribed muscle relaxers. The drug he took relaxed his heart.

My grandpa was there when, in middle school, the twin sister of my school buddy and friend disappeared. She was found three days later. Her burned body and remains 300 yards from the school. Grandpa, pop-pop always had an answer and it was usually simple and resilient. He worked coal mines in Pennsylvania and then, during WW2, was a rigger in a shipbuilding dock in south Baltimore. According to him, accidents happen all the time. Death was no different. In each case, we get up, brush it off, and then move on. After he died, I sat in a tree for about two weeks. Every day after school, I didn't do anything else. I had a little radio and drawing pads. After two weeks, my mom, his daughter, screamed from the upstairs window at me to get my dumb ass out of the tree. Time for moping around was over. Back then, we were not raised on therapy or talking. Action was the only answer. It is the first step.

I want to take a moment. There exists a pressure point system that works like a happiness hack for your body. You will take the first two fingers of your right hand and use them to add pressure to the inner wrist area on your left hand while seated. Controlling the context for this act is important. It is very important to only do this when seeing a sunrise, enjoying a good cup of coffee or tea or having a very special moment of joy. This technique has two purposes. The first is for you to sit or be present in this moment of happiness. Contentment. The second is to imprint it into memory. While seated, if possible, take the first two fingers of your right hand or dominant hand and press on the inner wrist area just up from your wrist of the opposite arm. Adding slight pressure, focus on this feeling, and do this repeatedly whenever you have a moment of happiness or accomplishment. It can be as simple as cleaning your living space. Sit and use your fingers to add pressure to this inner part of your left wrist. Now, if you must repeat this act each time you are happy or satisfied and do it over and over. There will come a moment in the future when you may get anxious or feel unsettled; you can take a moment and go to this wrist routine, use it and everything will subside. You will temporarily feel better. Gain some focus over your situation. This, I can say, works! However, you must remember to practice this little mental hack when you are happy and satisfied. It will also train you to be mentally aware of these moments. It will also take you out of stressful moments after building up good feelings over time. Practice, practice, and practice getting out of sad or depressive moods will take some time. The idea is to lessen the effect it has on our lives. We are taking action, the way through the maze.

Organize your space

You should now be cleaning yourself and your place regularly, and it takes less time to do when part of a routine. It is time to reorganize, rearrange or throw out things that no longer serve your interest. Change is our primary focus. One part of getting out of depression is wanting and accepting change. If just cleaning can make us feel slightly better, then keep doing it. Rearranging our living space can be a signal to our subconscious that we are ready to accept things new things that we were once unwilling to do. We were comfortable before. However, that broke down for some reason. At this point in time, we may not know the precise reason for it. So, let's take a little reasoning and put that into this new process of change. Personally, I love a good fire, and burning old furniture or a coffee table can be very satisfying. If you cannot build a fire, just donating or tossing out worn-out items can be just as good.

Make your bed:

I could have listed this right after personal hygiene, and this may seem silly, but your bed has been your only source of comfort. Perhaps this would be the very thing you do when you first wake up before your shower. Let's respect the part your bed has played in this past season. It is also one of the most used items in your living space. It's time to give it the respect it deserves, and most likely, the sheets need to be cleaned or changed. I only state that because I should change my sheets more often than I do. By making your bed every morning after rising, you have made your first accomplishment to this day. It is more than a functional ritual. It is a visual to yourself that sets an intention. That intention of today, I will not sleep this day away. Also, once you have made the effort to make the bed, you are less likely to hop right back in it. This is also the space you spend a great amount of time in. Keep it special, as if it is an oasis. It's these little steps that are the most beneficial towards recovery. We can't deny that, on some level, we need some help. Making your bed tells you and everything around you that you are ready to fix the problem. You are making a change, and you can control some aspects of your reality. There is another reason for this tiny 2-minute act. When you are finished with your day, and it is really time to go to bed, pulling back the comforter and climbing into that nicely made bed is like climbing into a cocoon of relief. It just feels different. Climbing into this nicely kept safe area tells your body to relax and tells your brain it is okay to sleep now. Better sleep is another step to a better you. This is a positive action, and each tiny layer reinforces our desire to thrive. Consciously and with attention.

Record your first day:

Bob Marley once exclaimed that you can not know your future unless you know your past. We all have experiences in our past that we want to remember and some experiences we really want to forget. There is no forgetting. There is only relief, and all things we would rather forget will need to be understood or categorized at some point. Recording our current state of living is part of a new start. It is these emotional experiences that need to be reprogrammed. At the very least, looked at from a different perspective. Most unresolved childhood issues remain only from a lack of understanding or forgiveness. I am not saying that some things are not forgivable when some form of abuse is the issue. Some traumas can last a lifetime. However, how we view them can be changed. What I am saying is that you are no longer the age or the person you were when these things occurred. Yesterday may have changed you forever. Today is what is important. Today, we have new knowledge. This very process you are reading may be new knowledge. If you do not have the understanding, then maybe it will take more investigation before it becomes an understanding. This may take assistance or may need a special amount of time to process. Regardless of the situation, issue or decision, there will always be only three choices we can make in life. The first choice is to accept it, the second choice is to change it, and the last is to leave it. Right now, your choice is to change it. You don't want to be depressed or sad any longer. Only you decide what is best for your situation; however, remember to forgive yourself if you are not in the desired outcome from a past decision or event. You are no longer that same person; you are changed by it. The person you were didn't know any better or didn't know there was another choice. If the situation was a death, then yes, the loss also has changed you. All that means is that person was a great influence and made you different in some way. It was a real connection. These are life lessons.

A healthy way to keep these issues or unsolvable problems is to write them down. A clear sign of depression is mental renumeration. The mental playback of stressful events or decisions that are causing us to stop living. To stop being present in your daily life. It is this failed attempt to make sense of something that we cannot process emotionally or logically that has contributed to our depressed state of being. Getting it out and putting it to paper will or can allow each of us the clarity and promise that I will examine this issue later. It buys us needed time. The very act of taking the time to write down our feelings and issues, our problems and concerns gets it out from the cloud of our mental body and into the realm of the 3d space in which we live. It is also through this very act that this particular set of emotions becomes real and not just something in our head. It is tangible. We cannot address any problem if we can not see past the effect it is having on our bodies. It is also one of the best and only healthy releases that will not have a negative impact on the very problem or thing we are stressing about.

Also, if we need help with something and cannot verbalize what is causing us pain, then when you can bring it to someone who can help, they too will be able to ask the right questions or provide the correct set of solutions. Journaling is a necessary component of your own self-healing. Perhaps the issue that is causing you to shut down is so emotional that you can't even tell if that is how you really feel about it. Has the situation been so overthought that it is a minor point of miscommunication or a symptom of an issue left over from some previous interaction from an experience totally outside of the current one? You just don't know until you can write it down. Put it away. Then, look at it with an unemotional state of understanding. Sometimes, more information may need to be gained to fix the issue. Once it is out of your head, relief enters.

There is a process that occurs when you journal, and sometimes, our current state of being is so dark that our flashlight may fail. By flashlight, I mean our vision to see clearly. Journaling is that light. It can be a spark to light a way through. We may stumble at journaling, forget to do it, and may have to restart. Journaling takes practice. Every part of this process takes practice. Learning to adulthood and learning how to take care of ourselves by ourselves takes practice. Daily practice. These steps are for daily activity. In time, they will become second nature. It is like muscle memory; repetitive action will take over until you no longer must think through the steps. Then, these habits will be a pattern of a learned activity.

So, what if you must start over? Sometimes, it takes years of repeated failures. There are times when we don't learn the lesson from a situation or repeated behavior that it repeats. Again, this is coming from my own experiences. Depression is something that never quite goes away for some people, but it can be transformed into just a moment of sadness. Yes, it can, and its effects will be less severe. Instead of days or weeks of depression, continually observed intention and consistent practice will eventually lessen our depressive bouts to a day or mere minutes of a day. Would you trade a depressive episode from years or weeks to mere minutes? I will take that trade anytime. Then, get serious about your recovery. Get serious about these steps. Get to writing out your thoughts. Get them out of your head so you can focus on your tasks that cover your daily activities. A small notebook. A sheet of paper in a binder, something! This is a necessary step to finding out what is going on. This is how you see yourself without having to ask someone else what they see. The life you save just might be your own.

The other side to journalling is that although everything in this beginning may seem overwhelming, you have already made progress. You will see the progress in your writing. By going through these steps in order and completing them, you change the outcome of your situation. In a brief period, you may find yourself sitting in the sun and thinking today feels good. It will happen without you realizing it. In that moment, congratulate yourself and if you can't remember how you got there or if things are starting to repeat even a little, go back and read how far you came. We can really celebrate if we know the things we overcame and read the steps it took to get there. If we can get to that point, then we may never, or you may never go back to that previous version of you ever. Why would you when the sun is better than the darkness? You don't know your future until you know your past.

A good start to a journal page might be as simple as:

-How do you feel?

-Why are you doing this?

-Write a rhyme or even a poem

-These pages are you being with you

Another way to start is if you are uncomfortable with your emotions now. Write that you are uncomfortable with your emotions. Write you think this is silly, but you are going to do it anyway.

-What is your vision for tomorrow?

-What are your spiritual Beliefs? If none, then maybe it's time to find them and start with that.

It is you writing to yourself. You are not recording this as an essay or assignment. It is you telling yourself and your future self that this is what today looks like. It is you saying, I am not okay today, and maybe that is all that comes out from your journaling session. I have used an entire page just with those words. The next part you should do is a daily journaling session around the same time each morning or evening before going to bed. It should be a period when no one is around to disturb you. Some days, you will write pages. Other days, it may be only a few words. Hopefully, when you are writing, the only words you say are, today was a good day, which can be enough. How wonderful is that very idea? Today was a good day. Journaling is also a way to measure another accomplishment. A way to feel good about something you took control of and made today better than yesterday. When we look back at the problems that seem so huge and we smile at who we have become, then we can make the next decisions in our life from a place of knowing who we are and not from fear or doubt. That is a kind of knowledge that cannot be replaced or taken away. It is these kinds of decisions that change lives. If your depression has caused some form of self-esteem issue, then guess what? You are taking action to resolve it.

*Repeat daily, be thankful, and give yourself credit.

My purpose for this exercise is to give guidance to the readers on the steps I have used to get out of heavy depression. For the longest time, and throughout my life, there have been overwhelming struggles and I have experienced things, some self-inflected and other things not of my own making, that have propelled me into dark emotions. Once a person has experienced a real struggle and gotten to the other side, they usually become very humbled or even kinder as a person. If only for no other reason than to not be the very person who caused them harm. I have caused harm to others not on purpose but from unhealed emotions of my own. Experiencing deep depression and years of just going through the motions of survival. I was not always able to have people or help groups around me for support. I was on my own and it was only up to me to solve or come to terms with my afflictions and struggles. I was, at times, arrogant and unyielding. Today, they call it narcissistic disorder. I believe I was just an egotistical ass. I learned the hard way; there was no way to live. Nor any way to live with yourself.

I was taught at an incredibly early age that I was to be thankful for everything I had available to me. I also forgot those lessons. There came a time in my life when I had to learn that having food, water, and a dry bed were comforts. Homelessness is a great way to learn humility and faith. Once those things are in good supply, then adding a roof over the head - everything else actually becomes a bonus. Being thankful and grateful has become second nature to me. The lesson has been well learned and understood. Everything can be taken away in an instant. It is not my intention to preach or overly extend my personal beliefs on these pages. Yet I am writing and speaking from experiences, and with that said, I must impart knowledge that there has always been an unexplainable presence in my life. My battles with depression and the dark emotions I have experienced and overcoming them are my proof of this supreme understanding. Many people that were once having been in my life are dead from the very experiences through which I have lived. Addictions and very poor coping choices have caused more suffering in my life than relief from the very issues that I was experiencing. People are no longer part of this world by suicide from having the very same emotions and deep despair that I have experienced in this lifetime. I, too, once took everything I was doing too far and overdosed. I am here to bear this burden and testimony that depression was in every part and that stage of my being. I have come extremely far from those days.

Depression is not the end. I am profoundly grateful to be able to extend these notions to you and to others. I am grateful each day when I leave my bed, make my bed, and get to start a new day. I give thanks, verbally and aloud, to whoever or whatever is listening. The life I live now is profoundly different from my life before. I found strategies and positive ways of coping with my life problems and lessons. The point is that the universe and the world we live in are strangers and mostly beyond our comprehension. So, with that humble acknowledgement, I profess that I am a small part of something bigger than myself, and I am grateful to the mechanism that governs over 'All That Is .' I give thanks for the chance to honor the life given to me today, which is better than the one I had yesterday. There has always been some form of guidance, and when I asked for help, it was given. Usually, in the most unexpected way.

It is up to you to also give yourself credit and thank you for doing the same. You have decided that today is going to be better than yesterday. These are the first steps out of depression. Say today, I chose to make my life better than yesterday. Now, give praise to the unknowable for guiding you, even if it is just a small voice in your head. Let's have fun with this! Be silly, laugh. We have spent too many days being serious; it's time to let it go!

Second Step

Second Step:

It's time to move your body. Stand up and twist. Shake your arms around, stomp your feet and wiggle. The action you need to take back control over your mood and thoughts can also be used to control your health. Depression contributes to lethargy and a lack of energy. The best way to combat that is to create movement. These simple steps will start activating all the stagnant areas of your body. You have been still and now is the moment of action. Any action will do, and it can only be for 15 minutes. I drive to my local gym and have an 18–20-minute playlist. I start it when I'm ready to get on the treadmill or use the machines to lift weights. When the playlist is over, I immediately stop. Will I become buff and build a flat tummy or prime physic? Maybe not, but I do it on a regular basis just to train my mind and my muscles to like it. To want it. I go for walks regularly, just to be outside. I do that regularly. Over twenty years ago, I started a program of tai chi, which evolved into the intentional movements of Qigong. It is like yoga with focused breathing and standard movements. These movements and continuous practice have opened doorways that I could not foresee prior to the practice. The benefits for my overall health cannot be measured.

Meeting others with similar experiences has led me to collaborate with others from around the world. This little program of taking time to exercise has propelled me far from the days clouded by depression, anguish, and sadness. It all started with 15 minutes a day. Mentally, my confidence and self-esteem improved immediately. Sometimes, I get really into it and watch my diet, but I don't have the expectation or any guilt if I fail one or two days of not getting to the gym. My Qigong practice is a daily activity first thing in the morning before I get distracted by responsibilities. I continuously find time to restart the gym practice simply because my body wants it. The point is just to get myself active enough that I would rather do those things than sit or sleep on the couch. It also keeps me active enough that I'm not thinking about much other than what I'm doing at the moment. Increased focus and clarity are all by-products of these activities. The surprise is I no longer think about doing it. It is now just a part of who I am. This program of steps is for that purpose. I know it all seems incredibly simplistic, but isn't that also the point? It was easy to fall into traps created out of grief or sadness. They, too, were simply little ways of coping with the trials of life.

The thing about depression is that prolonged grief becomes debilitating. It takes over your perspective and view of the world around you. It changes your self-concept and self-esteem. Your hope disappears and then everything turns grey. Not today! Today, right now, act. Take a walk and see how you feel afterwards. So many people make that New Year's resolution every year to get healthier. No one will push you to make a change like your parents did. Sometimes, the parents were an example of what not to do. That is an easy reason to make the decision to change. Do better for yourself, if only because you must live with yourself always and forever. I want to like what I see in the mirror, looking back. This wasn't always the case. Don't think about it; do something about it.

I have this new habit now that I really look forward to walking. I never know what different thing or person I will see while on my walk, and that's exciting. The idea of being actively outside and part of the world and not just existing in it feels revolutionary. It has become an inner strength that only by doing can someone fully appreciate. The gym habit comes and goes, but I'm not worried about it, nor do I think of it as an obligation. I am doing so many other things every day for my health that it compensates for this one extra desire. However, it's only 20 minutes a day, 3-4 times a week, and I have gotten stronger and more flexible. It's something that I personally and continuously must restart. It feels good, and subconsciously, it helps my self-esteem more. I do it for the feeling. I have this time for myself while doing it, and it clears my thoughts. The gym provides an additional little peace of mind, if only for a little while, but it's something I look forward to doing. It has added and given me hope. I still have bad days; who doesn't? Yet the bad isn't as bad, and the good is really good. If you will take the time to make your bed without much effort, and it is now a sacred space, shouldn't your body also be viewed as such? The outside you will become a reflection of the inside you.

*Repeat daily, be thankful, and give yourself credit.

I no longer struggle to do something healthy for myself, and that is an accomplishment. I got up, made my bed, took a shower, cleaned my space, and had Qigong and exercised a little. I write about it just so I know I am paying attention. I did those things and continue to do those things on my own, and I'm glad I did them. Nobody forced me to do it, and that is progress. I choose to do it. It's something I did for myself that I wasn't doing before, and today is better than the day before. I give thanks.

Third Step

Third Step:

Our next step is making our attention circle just a tad bigger. We have movement and a little momentum. Now, we can look at some of the other things going on in our life. I am purposely excluding some of our outside relationships, including those of our children. We cannot be there for anyone else until we show up for ourselves. The focus here is the issue of depression. We fix this and many of those other things will magically get in line and miraculously fix themselves.

-Work if money is an issue.

Do one thing that helps to improve your status. I started with work, and I consistently show up. I have mostly been a single person and could not rely on anyone else for money. When I was married, I still worked, if only to have the company of other people to talk with, which proved vital near the end of that failed experiment. I may not be the easiest person to cohabitate with; however, I was not the cause of that ending. Regardless, I could not improve upon anything without having the resources to do it. I could not pay my bills nor save for a better situation without working for it. The time I spend working is also the time I am not thinking or renumbering about my issues. The deceptive thing with depression is that we can function adequately and do our jobs and it sometimes hides our depression. This is not an optimal situation but a necessary functional one. It goes back to the notion of movement. We are attempting to keep the action in motion.

However, if you already do work or have a job and that is the reason you are depressed, then we need to investigate adding one or both other suggestions to our daily routine.

If you have an addiction, lots of drinking or drugs are causing you to be depressed or are contributing to chaos or some other unhealthy thoughts, habits and general upheaval in your life, then investigate the reading for step five prior to continuing this step.

-Sobriety, if not sober (Drugs, even prescription, falls under this heading)

Firstly, not all who suffer from depression have this problem with alcohol or substance abuse. If this doesn't fit your situation, then skip it. Only use or take what resonates with you. However, I have, and I understand and get this coping mechanism. I have been in pain, an emotional pain that never seemed to end. It became a daily routine. At first, drinking was just to relieve some stress from a long day of work and it was a highly intense work environment. IT worked for Pop-pop, my grandfather. He was a very early influence on many of my early habits. Remember, it was a very different time back then. Giving a four-year-old a sip of beer was a great way to put them to sleep so grownups could be grownups without the distraction. Drinking was a cultural norm.

My first job was in a restaurant and having a beer after work for a 15-year-old was really cool. I worked in high-volume restaurants for so long that it was how I lived, bust ass all day standing, and non-stop repetitive moment, then drinking all night. Hell, I had jobs where the first part of setting up my workstation was literally icing down cases of beer and making room for the bottles for later. However, events were also going on in my life that I did not take time to process, nor did I even want to spend one day emotionally shut down. I drank. Then, when drinking wouldn't do it for me, I added other things: pills, pot (marijuana), hallucinogens (mushrooms, Acid), cocaine, angel dust, whatever was available. What I mean by it wouldn't do it for me was that I drank to forget. To keep from the thoughts and emotions that kept rising from inside. I had loss and profound grief that I was taught to ignore. I had many friends die at an early age. I had a broken home life, and my father remarried with other children that I didn't really get along with and resented them having the family that I did not. All my support system of grandparents died, including some aunts and uncles, and an absent mother, and more death. All before I graduated high school. It was the death of one of my friends that really got to me. It was just after graduation, Woody. I was the black sheep in the neighborhood, and Woody was the one person we all looked up to. He was honest, loyal, and always helping everyone. He had a job working for a chain store, Murphy's Mart. It was like Walmart prior to Walmart. After graduation, he was promoted and trained to be a manager. A really big deal for someone in our neighborhood and something we all really admired and we were genuinely happy for him. He desired it more than anyone. He was a good person. He came home one day to change out the shocks on his car. Something we all in the group have done a million times over. He was alone, and the car slipped with the rear differential landing and crushing his chest. He died instantly.

After all the people I had lost, I could somewhat understand the circumstances. Old age, health problems, drug overdose or tragedy. I could no longer cope or understand the way someone like him, so deserving of a great life, had this happen to him. It sent me into a spiral and a loss of self-control. At 18, I was a full-fledged alcoholic and doer of every drug I could find. In two years, I had taken over 296 hits of acid and would have done more If only we didn't lose a ¼ sheet in a convenience store. I had a tribe of others all doing the same. Out of that group, there is only one other person besides me who I know of who is still living. I was depressed. I didn't care if I lived or died and I almost succeeded. I was given a second chance to change. I have fallen a few times along the way with drinking and smoking. However, I have made the most of what this life has given me. I have learned and studied the conditions and symptoms of depression. I know firsthand what the toll is and the price that must be paid for not addressing grief. I know how unresolved feelings and isolation can affect judgement and lead to ugly choices. I have seen firsthand friends die from the health cost of prolonged drug abuse. Depression is deceptive.

I remember on more than one occasion getting a phone call and hearing that someone close to me had died, then honestly taking a moment, smoking a cigarette, and then spending the next 8-10 hours cooking for hundreds or even a few thousand people. It is then that the coping mechanism becomes a crutch, and any sign of depression gets buried deep. Yet, it never goes away. It transforms into other forms of coping or added drug use with alcohol. All in a vain attempt to keep from having to feel. After a time, I forgot what I was trying to hide and acted out in many ways, like one-night stands, sex addiction, petty destruction, and general self-loathing. There comes a point when it can get so bad that you don't care if you live or die. That is the deception of depression, and when you do have downtime, the silence gets scary. When there are no distractions and you are all by yourself, and everyone needs time to yourself, the pain returns with a vengeance. It never goes away. You, at some point, must face and feel whatever has been tucked away, no matter how long. Sometimes, it's not just one thing anymore but a combination of things. The only solution at this point is to detox. Anyone who has had any type of long-term coping habit will tell you this is not an easy ride. It's a truth and a mirror you hold up to yourself and the realization that you are far away from the person you thought you were or recognized. It is not a good feeling and, in fact, compounds your depression. It is at this point that your body becomes numb, and all thoughts of happiness disappear. Get help! Call someone or a hotline. Doesn't matter who, what or where. Just talk to someone. Talk to the sky! Talk, scream… let somebody hear you. Then, ask for help.

The most popular choice these days is marijuana because of the lack of side effects, or the side effects are happiness, hunger, and sleep. It's a choice. The rub is that after prolonged use, your body does build a tolerance for the happy effects, and stronger varieties are needed to get into the desired state of being happy. At that point, it becomes another way of coping. It is an illusion and will require another detoxing period, which is just as harsh where depression is concerned. Perhaps you really don't feel like you have a coping problem, or your use of alcohol or drugs is only minor. Then test me. Test the whole idea that you are not suffering or hiding from depression. This can be your entire use of your journal. Go 90 days without anything other than non-alcoholic drinks. No weed. I dare you to go 90 days. Marijuana is an illusionary drug that can cloud your vision from seeing the things around you or the circle of people in your environment.

During this test of sobriety, see who stands by your choice and who shuns you. Prove to yourself that you are not in a depressed state and can make good choices. It takes a minimum of 30 days just to get most of the THC out of your system. This is the chemical that gives marijuana its high, and it is also the chemical that most affects the hippocampus area of the brain and regulates logic and emotion. Three months is one season during the calendar year. Afterwards, it's your choice. That is the main goal of this system, and these steps give you control over life. It is designed so you are in control and not your depression. If I am wrong about your particular situation and your depression was only a mild reaction to a single event, then, by all means, go back to your habits. If anything, it will provide you with insights to better yourself. Read your journal entries for the 90-day challenge.

It is times like these when a person can realize they are never truly alone. Who your friends really are. It is in times like these when miracles can happen. Unexplained phenomena, out-of-body experiences, and synchronicities. This is confirmation that your depression is not the end but can be the beginning of something better.

While it's not an official medical diagnosis, high-functioning depression is more common than most people think. That's because, as the name suggests, a person with high-functioning depression doesn't fit the "typical" profile that may come to mind when we think of someone living with depression.

People with high-functioning depression don't sleep all day, and their colleagues or family members might not suspect anything is wrong. Instead, "the struggles are often hidden behind success and productivity," explained licensed psychologist Natasha Trujillo.

Someone with high-functioning depression will probably not have issues performing well at work or fulfilling responsibilities at home. They may even use these productive actions to cope. Often, someone with high-functioning depression might not even know they're depressed at all.

So, what are the signs to look out for if you suspect you might be dealing with high-functioning depression? And what can you do about it?

Natasha Trujillo says the top high-functioning depression sign to look out for is that you don't experience any sustained sense of joy or pleasure despite good things happening.

"People with high-functioning depression remain productive, successful, and able to achieve," she said. "And yet, the person may not be able to maintain a mood of pride, joy, or pleasure for long, or they may pick apart a compliment or achievement to somehow make it 'less than' or inadequate in some way, emphasizing that they may not be deserving, or they just got lucky."

Therapist Becca Reed agrees with this. "Someone with high-functioning depression might feel disconnected as if they are going through the motions without genuine engagement or joy," she said. "This detachment can manifest as a lack of interest in activities they once enjoyed, a sense of being stuck in a routine or feeling emotionally flat even in situations that would typically bring about strong emotions."

Natasha Trujillo emphasized that there are other signs a person might have high-functioning depression. These may include:

- Forcing themselves to be social and go through the motions, even if they want to withdraw.
- Doing everything they're supposed to do but feeling like it takes more effort than it should.
- Having a hard time concentrating.
- Feeling fatigued, hopeless or worthless, even though they can't explain why.
- Feeling sad most of the time, with little or no relief.
- Changes in sleeping and eating patterns.

High-functioning depression is serious, and just as with more overt forms of depression, its consequences, if untreated, can include substance misuse and suicidal ideation.

In fact, someone with high-functioning depression might be at greater risk for suicide attempts because they feel so isolated in their experience, according to Saba Harouni Lurie, a licensed marriage and family therapist. So, getting help is key.

The first thing Natasha Trujillo encouraged is to work on being more open with loved ones about what you are experiencing.

"Being more vulnerable can help you gain support and connection," she said. "You can also work on focusing on what in your life isn't actually working for you and initiate ways to change what's maintaining your depression."

And, of course, finding help from a mental health professional should be a priority.

-Therapy, just having someone to talk to on a regular basis will ensure success

This will most likely be my most controversial entry within the context of this essay. I will start with the acknowledgment that I was raised in a generation of self-care. Meaning we had to take care of ourselves at a very young age and were mostly left alone. I was born in the mid to late 1960s and graduated high school in the late and early to mid-80s. No internet, no cell phones, no cameras, and no supervision. There was a reason the television shows had to remand parents at 9 and 10 pm, "do you know where your children are?" If something other than major blood loss occurred, we were expected to shake it off and deal with it. Bullies, we had to fight or were allowed to be beaten. We had no video games, so we had to create entertainment. Kicking the can was a very popular game back then. If you didn't have enough people to play football, you played a game of "smear the Queer." It was a game of tossing a ball in the air, and whoever caught it was chased and tackled. It could go on for hours. Everyone took turns. You were teased if you didn't catch the ball from time to time. We had no awareness that words can hurt, and genders were very specific. With all being said, Therapy was only for the criminally insane or very crazy people.

While I was in college for Sociology, I was exposed to many classes in psychology and quickly discovered that a large majority of students under that discipline were working to self-diagnose. I, for a while, was no exception. 0h, I did have issues and chronic bouts of depression. It did help and gave me new ideas or perspectives on how to view the things I have experienced in my life without guilt. It was a language tool on how to express things I could not comprehend. It was therapeutic. This was my first encounter with therapy. It helped. Up until that point, most of my emotional development and understanding of my outside world was based on spirituality or within the framework of religious-based ideology. Sociology also helped me expand that knowledge base to a more global awareness. Many cultures and many people have a variety of viewpoints and ideas; however, they usually come to the same conclusions. Language has always been a barrier to insightful understanding. This is where therapy can help any individual explain the things that they feel, yet they do not know how to express themselves.

Therapy should and can provide the safest space for people to trust that their issues are respected and are able to share without judgement. Trust is the main point. How can anyone expect to be vulnerable without trust? Relationships must be built upon it. Love cannot develop fully unless trust is its cornerstone. Group therapy is also an inclusive space when people feel isolated or as if no one understands their struggles. We all have struggles. Inclusion can be a valuable experience for people who feel isolated or completely misunderstood. We are humans, and we seek tribes. Groups of likeminded people for whom we can share the same ideas and feel inclusion. Tribes and these groups also provide areas where we can bounce off ideas and can be accepted or rejected without judgment. Groups should provide support if everyone is on equal footing and social understanding. Meaning we all know how to act in an agreed social situation. The overall purpose is to help us grow as individuals.

*Repeat daily, be thankful, and give credit.

If the work (job) we are doing is the cause of our depression, then continuing to show up is a reason to be grateful because you have more options available for yourself while you investigate the possibility of changing jobs. If changing jobs is not a possibility, then getting guidance is the next step. Also, once you have the experience of getting any type of assistance, be thankful. It is also important to use this time to embrace the possibility of miracles. It is in this area of the process that there can be a change in your perspective of how everything in your life will or has changed. Attempt to take some moments to reflect. You should have several pages written in your journal by now. Review; if not, restart the journaling. This is when you will really gain some momentum; it is also a point when we start to slack. Don't stop doing the things that are getting you to this point. Give yourself a little nod in the mirror each morning or in the evening to make today better than yesterday. Give an audible thanks to the sky or the air. Why not? I have another thought to point out. If you feel any sort of relief, even for a day, from taking these steps, notice it. Notice it. That will be a moment you will then be thankful to experience.

Fourth Step

Fourth Step:

Add one more thing from step three when comfortable until all three are part of your daily or weekly habits. This is part of the process and I talk of using small steps to get us out of depression. It may seem like just a continuation of the previous step; however, we are looking for consistency. A big part of this is getting our brains to accept these changes for maximum chance of success. When we are in a depressed state, we are not functioning, and our thoughts sometimes work against us. This situation is much harder to get a handle on if we have some unhealthy coping mechanisms. Those can be over-drinking alcohol or daily consumption of drugs. Prescription drugs are also a concern if they are anti-depressants or painkilling substances. Prolonged taking of these drugs masks the issues that only group therapy or non-group therapy can handle. Prolonged use of anti-depressants can cause other mental issues in addition to depression, known as BPDs or borderline personality disorders.

Now, at this stage, we are starting to look at the root causes of our depression. Also, at this point in this system, we should not have one or two newly established habits but several, and we no longer have time to just stare at the paint or the inside of our eyes. It is imperative that everything up until this point is profoundly and consistently a part of our daily lives. Again, it is my attempt to create an avenue or set of guidelines that we are in control of, and that is the point of this exercise. Taking back control over our thoughts and emotions so that we are no longer helpless against this phenomenon of fighting against depression.

Our days or weeks should look something like:

Keeping up on personal hygiene,

Making our beds,

Maintaining a clean space to live in

Some form of exercise or body movement, yoga

Daily journaling

Going to work

Maintaining a sober life purpose so that we can make clear and better decisions.

Counseling or maintaining regular therapy sessions to identify the root cause or causes of your depression.

And a daily practice of giving thanks to ourselves and the universe for assisting us in this process of creating a new version of ourselves.

It now seems like a lot of additional responsibilities when listed out, but it really isn't much at all when it becomes routine or second nature. Remember why we started? Review the notes you have in your journal. By this stage we can get well into the process. If not, then we know exactly where we are going. This is the roadmap to get us out of the darkness and into the sunshine. We can break this cycle of depression when we continuously review and add slowly. You are the conductor, the guiding hand in your recovery. You are controlling the outcome at each step. Nobody else is going to help you until they see you helping yourself. Others will notice the transformation before you notice it. It will not be easy, and you may have to start over a few times until things take hold, but it is better today than yesterday. That is our main objective. Make today better than yesterday. This is the map.

Another idea and addition to make is to do a craft or hobby in your downtime. If you have addiction or unhealthy habits, they get there because of idling. Not knowing how to overcome the spaces between activities. Depression is a symptom of something else within our mental framework. The people most likely to have severe depressive episodes are also highly intuitive and highly creative individuals. They also tend to learn at amazingly fast rates, can sometimes solve overly complex problems easily, and possibly have a higher capacity for above-average intellect. However, their ability to problem solve does not always equate to emotional stability. Also, mixing in an unhealthy dose of unresolved childhood trauma or wounding and then periods of downtime can be overwhelming for these personality types. Alcohol consumption or partying may seem a harmless way to fill in the time, but it is these very habits that create a base for depression to reside. The alternative is creating a healthy occupation or hobby. These hobbies can also be turned into a personal quest for owning or developing another source of income.

If the purpose of all these steps is to help ourselves and regain some sort of control system for our brains and regulate our depression into living a fulfilling life, then this is an easy extension of the process. We should also have some part in the decision-making process regarding what our new version of self will look like in the future. Adding an enjoyable hobby also helps us occupy the time that depression used to occupy.

*Repeat daily, be thankful, and give yourself credit.

These are all things we can control, and all steps will become second nature over a period. Continuous journaling will provide a reference to your thoughts and feelings each day. They will change over time and mark setbacks and success. Your journalling can also become a source for new ideas to flourish. If you are in any way practicing these steps for any length of time, then do something nice for a random stranger. Remember, a simple act of kindness can be the gift someone else needs to get through their day. You are learning how to refill your own vessel. Others will see it. Have the grace to share it with them. If it is your family, thank them for their support. Your growth shows them that they can do the same.

Fifth Step

Fifth Step:

Remove anything and anyone who stands in the way of the four Steps.

This may require a move of household, town, or may require a bigger change. Friendships or relationships can be the cause of your prolonged depression. This is a clean slate approach. Your history ends where you left it, and your new life and your new self await in a new place.

People will attempt to see you as you were and may not understand who you are becoming. Misery loves company, which means they may not want you to change because then they will have to change. You may not know who you are to become and an adjustment in scenery is all that may be needed to assist in your journey. This step can be a tricky one and is not necessarily a fifth step, but one that may cause some to consider prior to step two or step three. Only you can assess what is extreme or obviously necessary for your recovery. If you are in a serious drug habit or some relationship that is a cycle of bad choices, then this might be your step two.

Moving away from all that you currently know can be a huge decision. However, it just might be the right one to make only so you can get clean or into a situation that supports your recovery. It might seem scary at first, but starting from a clean slate will provide you with a visual landscape for which to build. A new place to live or a change of town can eradicate all memories and will cause you to completely focus on your tasks at hand. The requirements needed to find a new job, a place to live, and figuring out where to buy food and supplies will not leave you much time to wallow in self-pity. This is a drastic and far from easy step or choice. Yet, it might just be the one for you to find your tribe. A tribe is a group of people who are or have similar ideas that match your own. At some point in the process of learning about the root cause of your bout of depression, you will need support. People around you who will listen and assist in navigating the emotions and trials of recovery. This is particularly important when coming clean from alcohol addiction, or drug addiction is a concern.

There are so many avenues available: life coaches, therapists, group counseling, and centers for help. Hotlines are a place to ask if you need an honest direction to go. This is a time for reaching out. Asking for help is the bravest and most courageous of choices a person can make to make a change for the better. This also usually involves others who have experiences like your own, and they know what challenges you are facing or are about to face. Depression often isolates many people from the people around them and creates an illusion that you are all alone. Some forms of Functional Depression can also create a mental bubble in your mind that even if you are surrounded by people daily, you are not engaged nor emotionally capable of fully interacting with them. This form of depression is a hidden form of depression and can last years before you are able to recognize or are even aware of it. It is akin to being a walking zombie, and yet people only see you as an introvert or just a quiet person. These forms of depression are often triggered by the sudden loss of a loved one or a tragic event that is sometimes beyond reason or our understanding.

There are times when your whole life is interweaved with another person or even a group of people, and in an instant, they are gone. A car accident, an accidental death, or sudden disappearance can and do occur; it's a part of life. It hits you like a brick in the chest or a rogue ocean wave that you turned to face and didn't realize would knock you under the water and now you are struggling just to stand up, see what happened and even breathe. All you knew was this one person would always be there. Your tribe of friends and your closest family are now gone. It can take a few weeks just to clear up exactly what has occurred. There are even instances when someone just disappears without any explanation or reason given. They are all just gone. It is the sudden reality that you will never see them again, and you have no idea what to do about it, and life will never exist in the same viable way. That is a kind of void that leaves a hole in the middle of your soul. It is a sudden darkness that consumes all light, joy, and happiness. This is a depression that causes some people to end their own existence. It is in the strength of others that you can find comfort or guidance on how to fill this void. These few steps are how we get through the void and into a practical state of thinking and moving through it.

There also is another form of strength that can assist you past these agonies and troubles of life. Past the depressive state of being and the darkness. It only comes from a core foundation and is only built through time and practice. It starts with a firm belief in something greater than yourself. It is a vision and a faith of knowing and gaining by having an experience. An experience that only by walking through the darkness can a person attain. You must surrender all your ego or any thoughts. There is such a notion of being completely alone. We are more than the physical being that occupies this planet. We are a complex mechanism that contains an operating system that is us, and it regulates all our functioning. This is a blue spark of light and energy, according to some beliefs. However, the most recognized word for this operating system is soul. An unknown, unseen, but tangible feature created from vibration and frequency. It is an electrical impulse that causes consciousness and many abilities that we associate with thinking or cognitive functioning. It is also a tuning fork or antenna that receives and transmits vibrations and communication from an outside source. I will not dive into any form of religious discourse here, but I will state that I know it exists. I have felt it all my life. I know it exists because I am here. Writing these pages and passing along personal experience and the system for how I have gotten past my lifetime battles of depression. My very existence is my testimony that there is a force, a source, and an all-knowing something that has assisted me when others could not be there to help. I am grateful for the chance to experience another day of life. I am grateful because I can do better than I did yesterday. This one gesture is all that is required to place you on the path. Just give thanks. Be grateful. I consistently, without question, give my attention to this one thing. It is the least I can do, after so many others who have died or passed on in my life from making the exact same choices I once made, with the only difference being that I am still here. It is this act of giving thanks to 'all that is' that helps remind me of how far I have traveled and how many times I wanted to quit. Depression was the culprit for that form of thinking; quitting is depression in a nutshell.

I have not quit yet. I hope that you will also choose this mantra. Don't quit living today. Start with that, then go back to step one.

*Repeat these steps as many times as necessary. Be thankful and give yourself credit for doing the work. This is the greatest work we can do; our future self will thank you. Be Brave.

Conclusion

So here we are, and the choices are yours to make going forward. I included a quick reference guide of the Five Steps. Use that as a reminder and as a personal GPS device to move forward. I have outlined the things and steps that I have used to keep going forward in my life. I have stopped and restarted many times over, but I have always had to learn the lessons the hard way. I have also studied how and why I make the choices that I do, and every time I get a new piece of understanding, I apply it to the next thing I have to face. Continued study over your personal stuff could be step 6.

However, from this point on, this is your journey. I cannot know what you are exactly dealing with, and you are unique in how you process information. I have attempted to give you a tool to use so that you can make the best decisions possible, and it is up to you to either accept your situation, change it, or leave it. Once you get started, you may spend a few months or years understanding how and why you experienced depression, how you got to where you are and where you are going. There is no shame in it. I was once standing where you are and moved past it. After my darkest hour, I cleaned up, got into a very satisfying relationship and eventually went back to school. Somehow, despite all odds, I fulfilled a bunch of dreams and goals and graduated from college.

In the neighborhood I originally grew up in, it was an accomplishment to live and graduate high school. I faced my demons, and I am better for it. I continuously faced some hardships, but that is life. I look at it from a different perspective because I was different, and along the way, I continuously added new tools to my toolbox. This toolbox I refer to is the steps I use to examine an issue or an event from the knowledge gained from how I handled them before. These steps out of depression are your tools. Use them. Find more on your own to use. I am proud of the person I saw in the mirror today. I'm not a perfect person, and I still get down on myself when I make a mistake. However,

I do not let my emotions control my day. I control my emotions. I am in control of the decisions I make and my reactions to those arrangements or people around me. This is just the beginning of another adventure. Today is better than yesterday, and I am grateful for that. Thank you above, below, and in between for this gift, this life.

References

The Life-changing magic of tidying up, the Japanese art of decluttering and organizing

by Marie Kondo

10-minute declutter the stress-free habit for simplifying your home

by SJ Scott, Barrie Davenport

The Power of Less by Leo Babauta

https://www.huffpost.com/entry/sign-high-functioning-depression_I_664f53ebe4b01123ffe47664

This Is Depression: A Comprehensive, Compassionate Guide for Anyone Who Wants to Understand Depression

by Diane McIntosh

Overcoming Unwanted Intrusive Thoughts: A CBT-Based Guide to Getting Over Frightening, Obsessive, or Disturbing Thoughts

by Sally M. Winston PsyD and Martin N. Seif PhD

Biography

Who is Joseph Moore?

Qigong (energy work) Instructor

Bachelor of Sociology

Minored in Cultural Anthropology

Master's in religion

Doctor of Divinity

Explorer

Human

We all have a purpose and that is to be the best version of ourselves. We must accept ourselves as is for better and worse. We must hold ourselves accountable for our part in shaping the experiences that make up our lives. I have never stopped learning and consider myself a perpetual student. When I travel, that is my mindset to learn from wherever I am at any given moment. I understood a long time ago that even when traveling within the confines of the same state, there are always subtle differences, rules of conduct, and customs. I often think back to what it must have been like when America was first forming. The cultural differences and the challenges that languages, even within the same language, can be misinterpreted and how simple things can be completely misunderstood. That is the sociologist in me. Something I have always been about but didn't know what to call it or how to label it until a community college introduced me to the name sociology. The days and hours I have spent sitting on a bench just people-watching. Sometimes, I made up stories of what I was seeing. I am in awe of how it has continued to influence me despite the odds. Sociology is a methodology for examining every interaction through a lens of observation. Attempting to discern facts from fiction, truth from an illusion. When examining history and personal history, it amazes me how fragile the context of situations could have gone in myriads of ways and to my amusement and profound dismay, things always turn out just the way they were supposed to. Clarity is always revealed in hindsight. I would not be writing these pages if anything in the last few years were altered in any way. These are all events we need to connect to and then release. We cannot get overly attached to or fear any outcome in any situation. These are the lessons of our lives, and if we surrender to them as such, then we flow towards our highest good as if coasting downstream in a boat. The journey is the most important part. The destination is only a rest stop until the next journey begins. Never stop the exploration. I am supremely grateful for all I am. All that I have seen. Everything and all that I have felt. I am grateful to ALL THAT IS.